Wishing in the Wind

Written by Joyce Elaine Weber
Illustrated by A.M. Gerber

WISHING IN THE WIND

First Edition 2013

ISBN-10: 1-466-46004-0
ISBN-13: 978-1-466-46004-1

Illustrator's Website: www.AMGerber.com

Book Industry Standards and Communications (BISAC):
Juvenile Fiction / Stories in Verse

Library of Congress Control Number: 2013901568

Printed in U.S.A.

For Ella, Liam and Lucian Dorsey
and for every child of God

"Children's children are a crown
to the aged, and parents are the
pride of their children." Proverbs 17:6

- Joyce elaine Weber

To my Grandma,
who inspired me to strive for
a lifelong wish.

To my parents,
who have always said I could do anything.

To God,
who makes all things possible.

- A.M. Gerber

Sometimes I wish I were the wind,

I'd swirl the leaves and watch them spin;

I'd toss the kites and sail them high,

And blow the clouds around the sky;

I'd steer the sailboats smooth and swift,

And give a few folks' hats a lift;

And since I can't be seen, I'm glad,

I can't be blamed for being bad.

Sometimes I'd like to be a fish,
So I could swim just where I wish;
I'd glide along the ocean's floor,
From Newport News to Singapore;
My underwater world so free,
Has many wondrous things to see;
I'd stay away from hooks and bait,
And not end up on someone's plate.

Sometimes I wish I were a tree,
As big and broad as I could be;
I'd hold a swing for girls and boys,
So I could hear their happy noise;
A frisky squirrel might scamper up,
Or a kitten running from a pup;
On top I'd hide a robin's nest,
And furnish shade for folks to rest.

Sometimes I wish I were a bee,
Whose busy buzzing bothers me;
I wonder what he means to say,
Is it "Hello," or "Stay Away?"
Sunshine finds him near the flowers,
Where's he hiding during showers?
He seems happy making honey,
Even though he gets no money.

How fun to be a tall giraffe,
He always makes me kind of laugh;
His head's so small, his neck's so long,
But he's so graceful and so strong;
I wouldn't have to climb a tree,
To see as clear and far as he;
And boy, could I get places quick,
With those long legs to do the trick!

Sometimes I wish I were a clown,
Those times the circus comes to town;
I'd do some stunts upon a bike,
And act as foolish as I like;
Upon my face I'd paint a frown,
Wear baggy pants that tumble down;
Since seeking laughter is my game,
I'd make the children glad they came.

I'd love to be a kangaroo,
But not confined to any zoo;
Australia's where I'd want to be,
With many kangaroos like me;
My pouch is where my babies are,
As I'd leap high, and fast, and far;
But plants and grass are all I'd eat,
I'd miss my veggies, fruits and meat!

Sometimes I fancy I'm a plane,

That flies to France, Japan or Spain;

Across the oceans wide and blue,

To keep a scheduled rendezvous;

My passengers unload with cheer,

I watch them 'til they disappear;

On second thought, that's not ideal,

They leave me on the landing field!

Sometimes I wish I were a train,
That goes from Washington to Maine;
What fun to watch the gates go down,
As I go chugging through each town;
I'd shriek my brakes, then "All Aboard,"
A hustling, bustling, happy horde;
Or I might carry cars of freight,
But either way I'd be first rate.

Suppose I were a pumpkin seed,
Then sun and rain are all I'd need,
To push my way above the ground,
To soon grow big, and orange, and round;
Some friendly child would like my size,
And carve my nose, and mouth, and eyes;
Then with a candle placed inside,
I'd glow on Halloween with pride.

Just picture this: If I were King,
And had command of everything,
I'd have the biggest, best parade,
With fancy floats and lemonade;
We'd all obey the Golden Rule,
With more weekends and less of school;
I'd do away with being poor;
The country'd love me, that's for sure!

But mostly I like being me,

And not a clown, or train, or tree;

It's fun to be a girl or boy,

For there's so much that I enjoy,

And I like being tucked in bed;

I say my prayers and bow my head;

My mom says angels all applaud,

To know that I'm a child of God.

Made in the USA
Columbia, SC
14 August 2022

65323240R00018